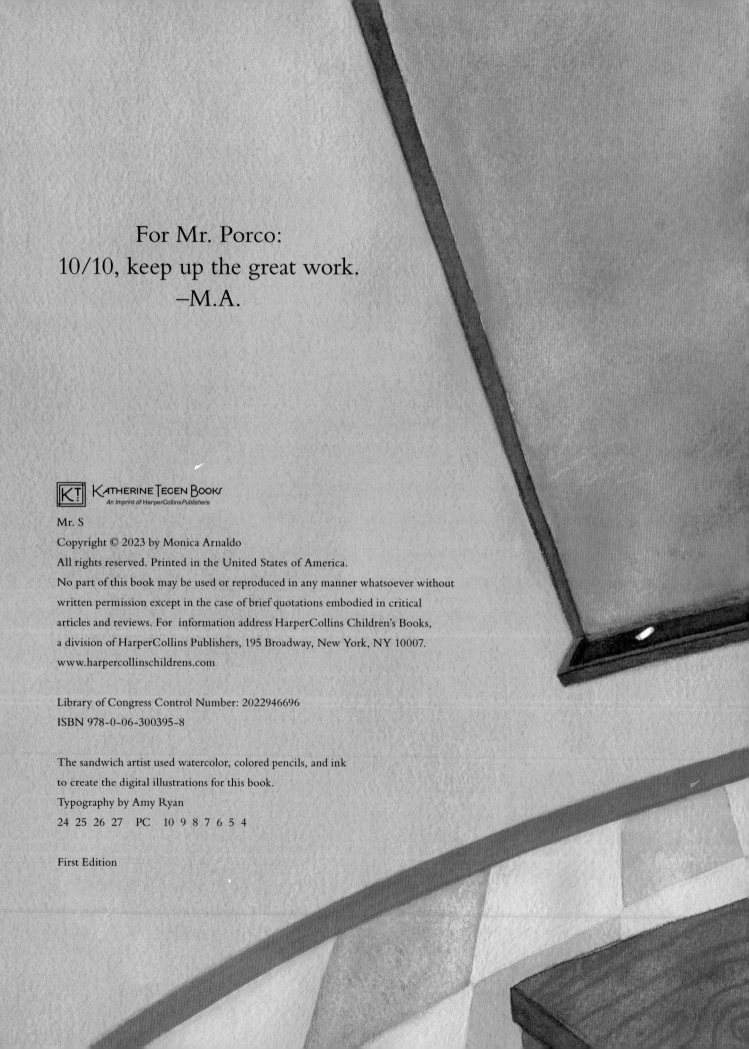

For Mr. Porco:
10/10, keep up the great work.
–M.A.

KATHERINE **T**EGEN **B**OOK*s*
An Imprint of HarperCollins Publishers

Mr. S

Copyright © 2023 by Monica Arnaldo

All rights reserved. Printed in the United States of America.

No part of this book may be used or reproduced in any manner whatsoever without

written permission except in the case of brief quotations embodied in critical

articles and reviews. For information address HarperCollins Children's Books,

a division of HarperCollins Publishers, 195 Broadway, New York, NY 10007.

www.harpercollinschildrens.com

Library of Congress Control Number: 2022946696

ISBN 978-0-06-300395-8

The sandwich artist used watercolor, colored pencils, and ink

to create the digital illustrations for this book.

Typography by Amy Ryan

24 25 26 27   PC   10 9 8 7 6 5 4

First Edition

The kids in room 2B could tell something was wrong. Even though it was their very first time at school, they had the sense that something was missing.

"Where's the teacher?" someone whispered.

"Shouldn't they be here by now?" asked someone else.

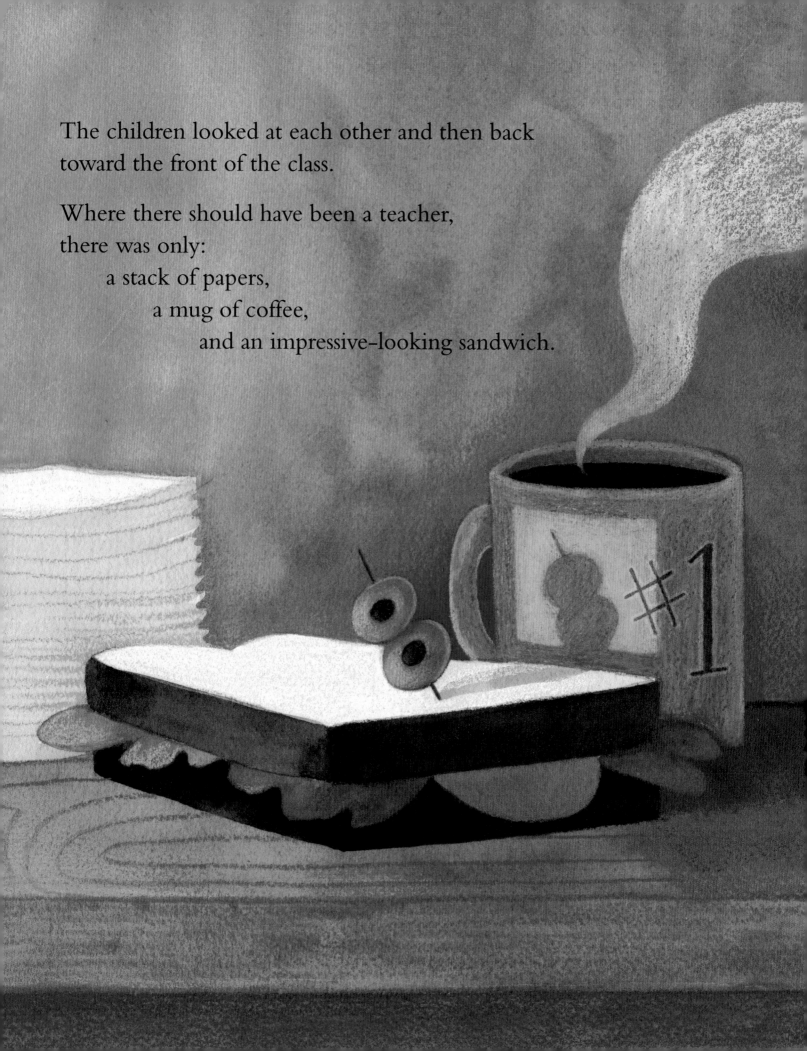

The children looked at each other and then back
toward the front of the class.

Where there should have been a teacher,
there was only:
        a stack of papers,
                a mug of coffee,
                        and an impressive-looking sandwich.

"No teacher means no rules!" cheered half the class.

"Absolutely not!" scolded the other half.

But before they could argue any further, a loud

THWACK!

came from the front
of the room, as a ruler
clattered to the ground.

"Who did that?" the kids whispered,
eyeing the teacher's desk nervously.

But there was only
the sandwich.

The clock ticked and the mug steamed,
but the sandwich lay remarkably still.

"You don't think ..." said one half of the class.

"...Don't be ridiculous," said the other.

"Look!" called a kid from the back of the room, pointing to the chalkboard.

There, written in perfectly neat handwriting, was a name:

As one, the children murmured:

That settled it.

Everyone got straight to work.

They moved swiftly through the day's lessons.

Mr. S was tough but fair.

The kids all loved art class.

Story time ran a bit long.

Music class was especially unconventional.

As the day went on, some students began to wonder:

The children argued quietly, and then not so quietly.

SLAM

Suddenly the door burst open.

The children in room 2B were perfectly silent as a very wet man made his way to the front of the class.

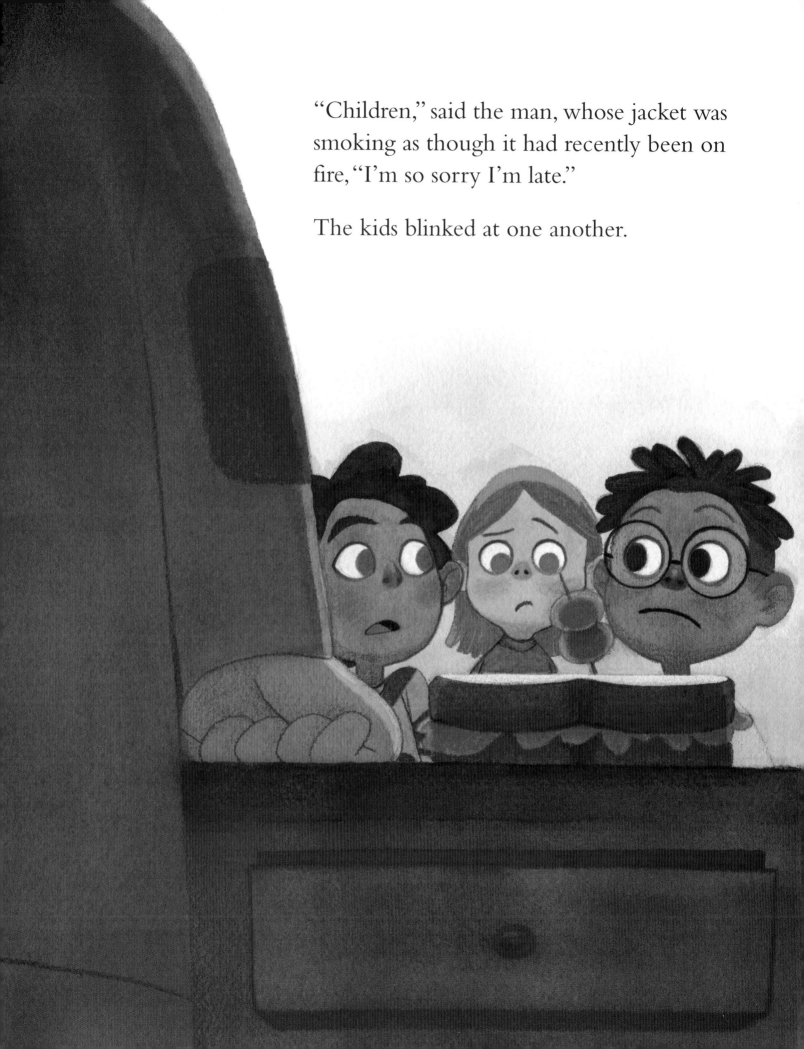

"Children," said the man, whose jacket was smoking as though it had recently been on fire, "I'm so sorry I'm late."

The kids blinked at one another.

"I've had an . . . unusual morning,"
he continued, "so I'm afraid we didn't
have time for a proper introduction."

The wet and smoky man picked up
a piece of chalk and began to write
on the board.

The children's eyes darted
            back
                and
                    forth
between the two figures at the front of the class.

"I'm

Mr. Spencer

Your . . ."

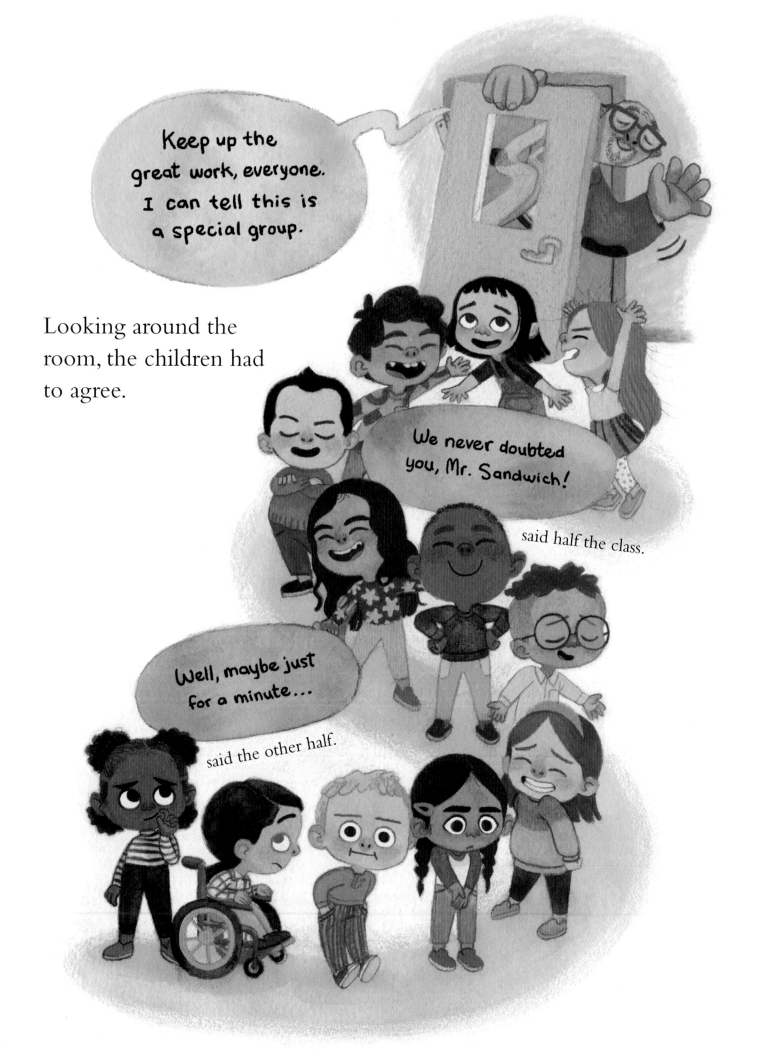

Looking around the room, the children had to agree.

said half the class.

said the other half.

Mr. S was as composed as ever.

"That's quite all right, children. But actually my name isn't Mr. Sandwich.

"The S stands for—"

avaliere

Ms. Hubbard

Mrs. Levick

ameron

Ms. Cho

Mr. San